Willard Douglas Coxey

Zenobia

A tragedy in three acts and eight scenes

Willard Douglas Coxey

Zenobia
A tragedy in three acts and eight scenes

ISBN/EAN: 9783337265069

Printed in Europe, USA, Canada, Australia, Japan

Cover: Foto ©Andreas Hilbeck / pixelio.de

More available books at **www.hansebooks.com**

ZENOBIA: A TRAGEDY

IN THREE ACTS AND EIGHT SCENES,

--AND--

A Confederate Episode

TOGETHER WITH

Five Wayside Rhymes

—BY—

WILLARD DOUGLAS COXEY,

Author of "Her Sacrifice," a Domestic Drama; "A Hypnotic
Crime" and "The Other Woman's Husband," and Co-
Author of the Anglo-Swedish Comedy, "Yon Yonson."

———

CHICAGO, ILL.

1897.

Characters in the Play.

DRACO, *an Athenian General.*

MARCIUS, *Draco's Ward, a Captain in the Athenian Army.*

DIOMED, *a Merchant, Father of Zenobia.*

PHILANDER, *a Privileged Slave.*

LEONIDAS, *a Young Soldier, Nephew to Draco.*

LYSANDER, *a Phœnician Soldier in the Persian Army*

ZENOBIA, *Wife of Draco.*

THEODOSIA, *Niece to Draco.*

LYDIA, *Maid to Zenobia.*

FIRST SOLDIER.

SECOND SOLDIER.

MESSENGER.

Judges, Soldiers, Citizens, Slaves, etc.

NOTE.--Although the battle of Marathon has been utilized as the background for the play, no effort has been made to be historically exact, either in the characters or the action. The critical student of history will also discover some very apparent anachronisms, which can only be excused on the ground of dramatic license.   W. D. C.

MAYWOOD, ILL., Feb. 15, 1897.

Zenobia : a Tragedy.

ACT I.

Scene.-Hall in Draco's Palace, Athens.   Time--490 B. C.

PHILANDER.

Women are puzzling creatures all ;
There's no philosophy can solve them.
                    (*Enter Lydia.*)
O, ho ! 'tis thou !   Oh-h-h-h ! thou fickle jade !
Where are the nectars, fruits and nuts
Thou promised me on yester eve ?
Methinks some other got my sweets.

LYDIA.

And I do think thou art a dunce.

5

Dost think me such a wasteful maid
To give such dainties to a fool ?

PHIL.

What's that ? a fool ?   More foolish she
Who speaks her mind without forethought ;
Who feels contempt, and shows it in her face.
They're wise who hate, and yet pretend to love ;
They nurture friends at trifling cost.

LYDIA.

Such friendships wither i' the making.
An honest maid does well to speak her mind.

PHIL.

Her mind? a woman with a mind?
Oh-h-h-h-h !   Here's meat for philosophy !

LYDIA.

I will be gone—I'll stay no more
To hear the babbling of a slave.

PHIL.

A slave?   Nay, twice a slave !
A slave to Draco and—to thee.
By Zeus, I'd have thee bear with me :
I'm not so ill-favored as I seem.

LYDIA.

Thy words would fret a goddess,

And I—I am anything but that.

PHIL.

Nay—'pon my soul, I did but jest!
Thou *art* a goddess—as fair as Juno,
And in wisdom like Minerva.
All women are goddesses.   In Draco's eyes
The drapery of his wife hides sprouting wings.
Oh, ho! an old god he to wed so late
So young a goddess.   In love, old men are blind;
Draco is doubly old, and doubly dull o' sight.

LYDIA.

What dost thou mean?

PHIL.   (*Singing*).

Six months wedded are Draco and Zenobia.
Draco loves the lady--the lady loves not "he."
Theodosia, Draco's niece, despised, is filled with jealousy,
   And e'en a witless slave can tell
That trouble's sure to be.

Ho! ho!   The world's a play
For such as we to laugh at.

LYDIA.

This is scandal.

PHIL.

Ay, scandal, with truth for a setting—
Fit gossip for generals' wives and archons'
   widows.
But of this we'll chatter more anon—

Zenobia : a Tragedy.

Thou art a sweeter morsel for discussion. (*Sings.*)

Oh, maiden fair, with the flaming hair,
Dost thou for Philander care,
An' wilt thou marry me?

(*He puts his arm about her waist, and she pushes it away.*)

LYDIA.

Nay, thou must not—an honest maid am I.

PHIL.

And I an honest man.
(*Kisses her. She feigns anger.*)

LYDIA.

Oh, shame ! I fain would hide my face.
I prithee let me go.

PHIL. (*Releasing her.*)

There ! thou art released.

LYDIA.

I—I would not be unkind. But
'Twere ill-luck to keep a kiss bestow'd by fraud.
I charge thee, take it back !

PHIL.

In truth will I, and that with eager haste.
(*Kisses her.*)
There, thou hast good luck again,
And I, sweet maid, have a pair of kisses.

8

Zenobia : a Tragedy.

(*Enter Zenobia and Marcius from centre.*)

MARCIUS (*Laughing*).

Heigho ! another fool in love !

ZENOBIA.

What ! hast thou been to the philosophers
That thou hast become a cynic?
Ah, good Marcius, he's not so much a fool.
Besides, 't is nature—let's give our blessing :
More women marry fools than wise men.

PHIL.

Thanks, my lady, thanks.   (*Sings.*)

> Oh, tender the heart that loves, itself—
> It judges others kindly ;
> Old age and youth are wed in vain
> When lovers go it blindly.

ZEN. (*aside*).

What means the slave?   Can he suspect?
(*Aloud.*)   Philander's in a merry mood.

PHIL.

Twice merry, my lady—why not?
Within the bonds of General Draco
Am I not a slave?—and yet
I've won a maiden's heart.   Mark you, a maid !
I make no love to wives.
(*Aside, as Zenobia starts.*) That reached the quick.
(*Exits centre, bowing.*)

MAR. (*aside*).

This fellow's words have double meaning.

Can he think I am Zenobia's lover?

ZEN. (*to Lydia*).

Blushes become thee—
And yet thou art young to be in love.

LYDIA.

In love, my lady? Nay,
Thou didst but interrupt a game.

MAR. (*laughing*).

A game? Heigho! a game?
By all the graces is her meaning plain.
She angles for the slave, and then of him—
    makes game!
Who says that coquetry is a thing of station?

ZEN.

Well said, good Marcius—but enough of merri-
    ment.
Go, Lydia, and say to Draco, my lord,
I will be with him presently.

(*Lydia exits, left. Zenobia reclines on couch*)

Repose thyself, Marcius—I wish to hold
Serious discourse with thee. My heart is heavy,
And I need the sympathy of honest friendship.
    ——Thou art my friend?

MAR. (*Sitting beside her.*)

Thou art Draco's wife. What's dear to him
Shall ever claim my loyalty.

Zenobia : a Tragedy.

ZEN.

On yester eve I spoke to thee of one
Whose love I hold more dearly than my life,
And yet whose name I dare not speak in Athens.
Of this dear one I fain would tell thee more,
But first, upon thy honor, must thou pledge thy-
  self,
In payment for my confidence, to keep my trust.

MAR.

I am already pledged—
Let all the gods be witness to my oath !

ZEN.

My father is by birth a Phoenician :
I, myself, was born within the walls of Sidon,
That city which, they say, the gods did build.
I had a *brother*—
A manly, noble youth—a nobler man.
He loved beneath his rank.   My father, deep-
  incensed,
Cursed him, cast him off, and swore
His eyes would never look upon his face again.
Lysander went away, and I, a child,
Wept for many a weary day, because I loved him,
Loved him more than sisters often love,
For all our early life was spent together,
With never one to come between us.
For years
My heart has yearned to see Lysander's face,

To press his hands, to look within his eyes
And read the loving spirit that I knew of old.
But this has been denied.
My father, now become a citizen of Athens,
Lest he make his standing insecure,
Denies his only son ; while Draco,
Who doth still believe my mother was a Greek,
Has naught but scorn within his heart
For all who own the blood of dark Phoenicia.
    —Thus have we been kept apart.
To-day I learned my *brother* was at Marathon.

MAR.

Thy brother at Marathon?

ZEN.

Alas ! in the Persian army.

MAR.

Among the soldiers of the invader !

ZEN.

'Tis true—among thy enemies
And the enemies of my adopted country ;
Yet does my soul cling to him
With all the tender yearning of a *sister's* love—
Courting all danger—braving all condemnation,
That I may see my *brother* once again.
    Good Marcius, thou wilt aid me?

MAR.

I would, my lady, but——

12

Zenobia : a Tragedy.

ZEN.

Thou dost not fear——?

MAR.

I never knew the meaning of that word till now ;
And yet I have no dread of danger or of death ;
It is disgrace that frights me most.
To aid thee must I be false to Draco.

ZEN.

No, no, Marcius, I would not have thee be untrue
Either to thyself, thy country, or to Draco :
Still, thou art a soldier, and a soldier's cunning
May find the means to aid a helpless woman
Without treason to the cause he loves.
    Sweet friend (*caressing him*),
Thou art my only hope —thou wilt not say me nay!

MAR.

Almost dost thou persuade me—and yet—
And yet is my conscience ill at ease.

ZEN.

Thou canst make me happy if thou wilt.

MAR. (*Rising.*)

What wouldst thou have me do?

ZEN.

  Enter the Persian lines. Find Lysander
And guide him hence. A good disguise,
And bravery such as thou, I know, possess,

13

Are all that's needed to complete the task.
(*Rises, and seizes his hands.*)
Marcius, bring thou here to me my *brother*,
And thou shalt have my everlasting gratitude !
—Say thou wilt do this for me !

MAR. (*Aside.*)

My judgment tells me that I err ; but when
Did soldier ever fail to play
The gallant to a woman's tears?
(*Aloud.*) I'll do it, Zenobia ; tho' it cost me dear,
I'll bring to thee thy brother here !

ZEN.

Ah, my good, my noble friend,
I knew thou wouldst consent.   But when—
When shall I see Lysander?

MAR.

To-night—if so we do return to camp.
Trust me, Zenobia, thou shalt see thy brother.
But now, farewell—thy husband comes,
And for a little space I would not meet him.

(*Hurriedly presses her hands, and exits centre.*)

ZEN. (*Resuming her position on couch.*)

Ah, me! I must be calm,
Else will I betray myself, and all my scheming
come to naught.
Lysander, dear, this very night, if all goes well,
I'll see thee once again—feel thy arms about me,

14

Thy kisses on my lips.   Yes, Lysander,
Thou art, for this brief time, my *brother!*
To-night, I'll call thee what thou art—my *lover!*

(*Enter Draco, left.*)

DRACO.

Zenobia!   (*She does not answer.*)   Zenobia.

ZEN. (*indifferently.*)

Yes, my lord.

DRA.

Thou art not thyself to-day—nor hast thou been
For a month or more.   Art thou ill, Zenobia?

ZEN.

No, my lord.

DRA.

Or unhappy?

ZEN.

No, my lord.

DRA.

I would I had thy confidence,
That I might share thy thoughts with thee.—
Hast thou wearied of thy aged husband?

ZEN.

Why dost thou ask that
Which thou canst better answer for thyself?

DRA.

Six months and more have we been wed,

15

And still I feel thy heart does not respond to mine.
Canst thou not love me, Zenobia?

ZEN.

Why wilt thou weary me?   I—I love thee.

DRA.

Thy words doth lack the fire of fond regard,
Else am I foolish—made childish by my love!
They say, old fools are young fools thrice over.

ZEN.

I love thee ;—what more wouldst thou have me
    say?

(*Rises, and walks to centre. . Draco follows and
    attempts to caress her.   She draws away.*)

DRA.

I would not be unjust—and yet
Thou hast a strange way to show thy love.

ZEN.

Still do I love thee.   Be content ;
And if thy love for me is such as thou doth still
    protest,
Leave me to myself; that— I may think of thee.

(*Permits him to kiss her.*)

DRA.

Now thou art thyself again!
Had every day a gift for me so sweet as this,

Zenobia : a Tragedy.

I'd live a thousand years, and every year
Would forge a stronger chain
To make me more thy slave.—
Ah, Zenobia, am I not favored of the gods
To have thee for a wife?

(*Hastily seizes her hand, kisses it, and exits right.*)

ZEN.

Love him?   With all my soul I hate!
A woman never loves but once,
And tho' my husband claims my hand,
Lysander has my heart!

(*Enter Lydia, centre.*)

LYDIA.

Quick, lady, quick!—thy father hast returned!

ZEN.

My father?   Then must I prepare for him!

(*Both exit, centre.   Theodosia and Leonidas enter
from left.*)

LEONIDAS.

Wilt thou not rejoice with me—a captain?

THEODOSIA.

Hail, Captain Leonidas—hail!
Indeed, the title suits thee well.   For thy sake
I would 't were nothing less than general.

LEON.

And I, for thy sake, would it were a crown,

17

That I might dare to lay it at thy feet,
Fearing not to call thee queen.

THEO.

Thou art a foolish boy.   Say no more—
One victory's enough to-day.

(*Enter Marcius, centre.*)

Good Marcius, what troubles thee?

MAR. (*Smiling.*)

Not thou, sweet cousin.

THEO.

When dost thou return to camp?

MAR.

Perhaps to-night.
The Persian hosts have left their ships,
And on the plain of Marathon
Prepare to give us battle.—
Before another day has passed
We'll drive the tyrant to the sea,
Or say farewell to Athens.

(*Marcius and Theodosia walk to left, and speak confidentially.*)

LEON. (*Aside*).
'T is Marcius she loves!
How every action speaks the thought within her
mind.
I will be gone—I dare not stay

Zenobia : a Tragedy.

Lest all the jealous hate within me rise
To do them both some injury. (*Exits right.*)

THEO.

I'm no less brave than other women are,
And yet I fear the issue of this war.
The lives of those I hold most dear
    Will be in peril.

MAR.

Thou needst not fear for Draco. His single arm
Is strong enough to put to flight a thousand
    Persians.

THEO.

My uncle? Yes, I've heard it said
A braver soldier never in all Greece was known ;
And tho' I do respect him much,
I've other, dearer friends than he.

MAR. (*Laughing*)

I did forget Leonidas.

THEO.

Leonidas, indeed! Now dost thou jest—
A pretty, clever boy—I like him much—
He is my cousin—nothing more.
Canst not think of others, nearer, dearer yet?

MAR.

I know there is no other maid in all fair Athens
Whose friends are numbered by so many score :

Indeed, I've often envied those who call thee so.

THEO.

And thou dost call thyself a soldier,
To envy that which daring never failed to win—
        A woman's friendship?

MAR.

Then might I dare——?

      (*Enter Zenobia from centre.*)

THEO.

Hush——!

ZEN.

Good friends, I did expect to find you here,
And in that expectation came to bring good news.
My merchant father hath returned to Athens.

MAR.

Comes he from Tyre?

ZEN.

So am I told ; and brings new slaves, rich jewels,
Women's goods from Persia, Indus spices,
And pretty gawds to tempt the vulgar herd of
      Athens.   (*Commotion outside.*)
'T is he! Diomed comes! Oh, lucky day
That brings my father safely home!
Behind the curtains will I hide until he call me.

(*Secretes herself behind curtains, left.   Draco and
      Diomed enter from centre.*)

Zenobia : a Tragedy.

DRA.

Welcome to Athens, tho' thy coming
Is ill-timed.   A soldier may not play the host
When duty calls him to the camp.
   —Still, thou art welcome.

DIOMED.

I thank thee, Draco. But where's my daughter?

ZEN. (*Advancing from curtains.*)

Here am I, father!

DIO.

Zenobia, my child!   (*Embraces her.*)

ZEN.

'T is sweet to see thee—sweet to know
That, dangers past, thou hast returned.
—Good sire, I pray thee go no more.

DIO.

Nay, and I will not.   This voyage
Hath well enriched me.   'T will be my last.
My bones begin to feel the touch of age ;
I'll stay, and my daughter shall see more of me.
   (*Turns to others.*)
   Forgive me, friends, but
With my daughter I would speak alone.

DRA.

Thy wish shall be respected.

Zenobia : a Tragedy.

Come, Marcius—and thou, my niece.

(*Draco, Marcius and Theodosia exit centre. Diomed seats himself.*)

DIO.

Come, Zenobia, kneel beside me here,
Where I can read thy heart.   (*She kneels.*)
Six months have passed since last I saw thee ;
Then thou wast a new-made bride ;
Now thou art a full-fledged wife.

        —Thou art content?

ZEN.

Content?   What mockery to ask!
Can youth enchained be e'er content?

DIO.

Why dost thou speak in riddles?

ZEN.

        Then will I be more plain.
Father, I hate this man !   Against my will I
    married him.
'T was thou who forced it.   I loved him not—
I cannot love him now!

DIO.

Thy words doth grieve me much.
I never thought to hear thee thus berate thy sire.
Go! Thou art an unfeeling child!
    (*Pushes her away.   She clings to him.*)

Zenobia : a Tragedy.

ZEN.

Forgive me, father. 'T is wrong for me to speak,
Still, is it in my mind, and what's within is better
    out.
For thy sake have I tried to love him,
Yet he doth but grieve my heart. (*Weeps.*)

DIO. (*Aside.*)

The leaven works! She'll break the spirit of
    this haughty Greek,
And bring disgrace upon his name.
I love the nymph, and yet revenge is far more
    sweet. (*Aloud.*)
Weep not, my child. Thy duty is to Draco—
See that thou doth fail him not.

(*Enter Draco and Marcius, centre.*)

DRA.

Still here? I would necessity
Had not compelled us to intrude.
    —A word with thee, Diomed.

(*Diomed and Zenobia rise. Draco and Diomed
walk to left, and Zenobia and Marcius to centre.*)

ZEN.

Thou wilt not forget, Marcius?

MAR.

I will not fail thee.

23

Zenobia : a Tragedy.

ZEN.

Thou little knowest the service thou wilt do me;
I cannot pay thee as thou wilt deserve.

MAR.

Thy gratitude is reward enough.

(*Messenger rushes in and hands Draco a paper.
Draco steps apart to read it.*)

DIO. (*Looking at Zenobia and Marcius.*)

So! 't is this young Greek who holds her heart!
Her love for him shall be the means
I'll use to undo Draco!

DRA. (*Reading letter.*)

How's this?   Word from Miltiades?
The plan of battle has been formed,
And ere to-morrow's sun has set
We'll try our strength with Persia.
—Diomed, thou wilt pardon us—we must away!
(*Turning to Marcius.*)
We must to camp at once!   Prepare thyself,
And, within the hour, meet me in the portico.

(*Draco turns to Diomed.   Zenobia reaches out her
hand to Marcius, who kisses it, and hurriedly
exits, left.*)

DRA. (*to Diomed.*)

The fate of Attica rests upon this battle,
And failure means the loss of Athens.

24

Zenobia : a Tragedy.

Stay thou here, and, should I fall,
Remember, all I have is thine in trust
For my dear wife, Zenobia.

Dio.

With me thy wish is law.

Dra.

Then—farewell.   (*Clasp hands.*)

Zen. (*Aside.*)

Oh, Lysander, dear, if thou shouldst fall,
And I should never see thy face again,
Death might find me here and welcome!

(*Draco approaches Zenobia, and Diomed secretes
himself behind curtains, left.*)

Dra.

Why dost thou weep, Zenobia?

Zen.

For dread of danger to my love.

Dra.

Thou dost weep for me?

Zen.

Ay, for my love.   Go!   The gods defend thee!

Dra. (*Embracing her.*)

Farewell, sweet wife!

Zen.

Farewell.   (*Exit Draco, centre.*)

Zenobia : a Tragedy.

The blind old fool ! What right
Has he to think himself my love?
Mercy 't is he's gone! I scarce
Could all my hate contain,
And in my fury might have ruined all.

Dio. (*Looking through curtain, rubbing his hands.*)
She loves the youth!—she loves young Marcius!
Soon shall I be revenged !

Zen. (*Throwing herself upon the couch.*)

I pray the gods the battle's not to-night,
For so will Marcius bring to me my love.
Be still, my heart, and trust in fate—
'T is but a little while to wait,
And then, if fortune doth betide,
I'll have Lysander at my side!

END OF FIRST ACT.

Zenobia : a Tragedy.

ACT II.

THEO. (*Entering from left and seating herself on rustic bench.*)

What secret understanding can there be
Between Zenobia and Marcius?
I watched them as they bade farewell,
And all the jealous rage within me woke
To see her smile adieu!
'T is court'sy overdone—such sweet farewells
Are only meet for lovers' partings.
(*Enter Diomed, right.*)

DIO.

Who's this—Theodosia?
Dost thou enjoy the evening air in solitude,
When lover's nonsense might, forsooth,
Beguile the passing hour?   Where's Leonidas?

THEO.

I know not—'t is not for such as he

Zenobia : a Tragedy.

To waken thoughts of love.

DIO.

Forgive me—I would not willingly offend.
I have seen you much in company,
And did think you were betrothed.—
An old man's want of tact—naught else.
    —'T is Marcius you love!

THEO.

. I would not speak of that.

DIO.

Then, 't is true—thou lovest Marcius?

THEO.

He loves not me.

DIO.

Still, thou dost love *him?*

THEO. (*Aside.*)

Why should I fear to speak?
(*Aloud.*) I do—with all my soul I love him!

DIO.

And he loves thee not?

THEO.

Alas! I thought he loved me once.

DIO.

Perhaps he loves thee, and hesitates to speak.

Zenobia : a Tragedy.

THEO.

I fear another has his heart.

DIO.

And she——?

THEO.

It were unmaidenly to speak her name—
Thou must not ask me.

DIO.

I know the truth already!
'T is Zenobia—my daughter—Draco's wife!

THEO.

Thou sayest truly—'t is Zenobia.

DIO.

And she returns his love?

THEO.

Thou art her father—I would not speak.

DIO.

And I would have thee tell the truth.
This thing hath much interest for me.

THEO.

Well, then—I did believe she loved him.

DIO.

I know it! What's more,
I know that here, within the hour,

They'll meet again and pledge their secret vows.
'T is but two hours from the camp,
And Marcius will find some pretext to return.

THEO.

They'll meet, and here?   The thought
Is maddening!   And yet, why should I care?
He loves not me.

DIO.

Under these very trees he'll speak his loving
      words,
And she will rest upon his heart!

THEO. (*Excitedly springing to her feet.*)

Ah! why dost thou torture me?

DIO.

Because it is a wanton insult!
He makes your love a passing jest,
And flaunts my daughter's weakness in my face!
Were I a woman, and thus betrayed——!

THEO.

What wouldst thou do?

DIO.

I'd have revenge, altho' it cost my life!

THEO.

And so would I—but what
Can women do when thus depised?

Zenobia : a Tragedy.

Dio.

Listen.—
Let us secrete ourselves by yonder bush ;
There will we wait and watch, and with
Our very eyes behold the lovers meet—
Drink to our fill of hatred, and then
While I remain to guard my daughter,
Thou shalt away to camp to tell the tale to Draco,
And bring him back to witness their intrigue!
Thus shalt thou be revenged !

Theo.

        A fury's in me!
Love is sweet, but sweeter still 's revenge!
I'll do it!   Let's wait, and, if 't is true—
If Marcius and Zenobia meet—
Love shall not stay me, but jealous rage
Shall speed me on my errand!

Dio.

Hush!--someone comes--let us retire.

(*Theodosia and Diomed retreat behind bushes, left.
Zenobia enters from right.*)

Zen.

It is the hour, and this the place ;
'T is here Marcius promised to bring Lysander.
The gods grant no mishap may befall them,
For delay is torture, and moments, while they
    come not,

Seem like leaden hours.   How still's the night!
The air is heavy, and a fearful dread
Rests on my heart. What if Marcius is betrayed,
Or Draco has divined the truth!

    Oh, foolish heart!
It is a woman's way to think of ills
When naught but happiness awaits.
They'll come—I know they'll come—
Lysander loves me far too well
To tarry when I bid him hence.

    Ah, Lysander!
It were a crime to love thee—yet
My heart can love none else.
Thou art my life, my soul, my other self—
I cannot live without thee!

   (*Nightingale sings.   Zenobia listens.*)
    What's that?   Marcius?
Nay, 't was but a nightingale on yonder bough.
Sweet songster of the night, I pray thee
Sing again and give me courage!
    Why do they stay?
Good Marcius, I wait thee—come,
And with thee bring my love, Lysander!

   (*Enter Marcius from centre.*)

    MAR.

Zenobia!

    ZEN.

Is it thou, Marcius?

     3₂

Zenobia : a Tragedy.

Mar.

Yes, 't is I, Zenobia.

Zen.

The fates be praised!   I 'gan to think thee false,
Or else that fortune had betrayed us.

Mar.

That were a cruel thought—
I have risked much to aid thee.

Zen.

I know thou hast ; forgive me ;
In my heart I knew that thou wert true. —
But, where's my *brother?*—where's Lysander?

Mar.

In the shadow of yonder wall.
I feared to bring him here lest his garb betray him.

Zen.

Good Marcius, thou art the best of friends,
And thus I show my gratitude.

(Impulsively kisses him.)

Thou hast this night a kindness done me
That I will well repay ; but now, I pray thee,
Take me to Lysander.   I am all impatience,
And would see my *brother!*

Mar.

Then come ; 't is but a step away.

Zenobia : a Tragedy.

Thou shalt speak to him alone, while I
Will wait within the shadow of the trees.
When thy brother's ready to return
A signal will recall me.

(*Exit together, centre.   Diomed and Theodosia
enter from left.*)

DIO.

Did I not tell thee true?

THEO.

Alas, he loves her, and my heart is scorned!
Let's watch a little longer—then I'll away ;
Revenge shall give me strength !

DIO.

Lead on—I'll follow.

(*Theodosia cautiously exits, centre, followed by
Diomed.   Zenobia and Lysander enter, right.*)

ZEN.

Lysander, dear—art thou in truth Lysander?
And am I Zenobia?   Do I but dream,
And is this thy shade, and not thyself,
That holds these arms about me?
Kiss me, my love, that I may know
Thou art a substance, by the pressure of thy lips.

LYSANDER (*Kissing her*).

It is no dream.
Thou art my own Zenobia, and I, Lysander!

34

Zenobia : a Tragedy.

These arms that now embrace thee
Are the arms that held thee long ago
In that sweet time when all the earth
Was filled with joy, and all the flowers sang,
Because the gods had joined our hearts.

ZEN.

And is thy love for me, Lysander,
As deep and true as in those vanished days,
When every loving speech of thine
Was a vow of everlasting constancy?

LYS.

Deeper, by far, Zenobia; for then I was a boy,
And, with the fickle fancy of a youth,
A face more lovely than thine own—
If such a one in Sidon had been found—
Might then have wooed me from thy side;
But parting made me what I am to-night—a man!
And tho' thy father, apostate as he is,
Renounced his country and became a citizen of
     Athens,
And by that self-expatriation hoped
To cut the bonds that bound thy heart and mine,
In all the passing years my heart has held
But one sweet image—thine!
                    Without the missives
Fondly writ by these dear hands,
I should have grieved my heart away,
Or, in desperation, risked my life,

And come to thee in Athens.

ZEN.

And now thou art here.

LYS.

Yes—with thrice ten thousand
Of thy countrymen and mine.

ZEN.

Soft!—thou wilt be overheard ;
All here think I am a Greek.

LYS.

And what if they knew else?

ZEN.

Why—my husband——

LYS.

Thy husband——?

ZEN.

Yes ; dost thou not know I am the wife of Draco?

LYS.

A wife?   Thou a wife?
Ah, Zenobia, how quick thou didst forget me!

ZEN.

Hush, my love!

LYS.

Thy love?   Nay,

36

Zenobia : a Tragedy.

Never more will I be love of thine!
Why didst thou bring me here?
Was it to tell me this—that thou,
The woman whom I loved—
Whose face has been my guiding star
On many a bloody field of war—
Pledged to be mine, by all that's good above
And all that's pure below—
Is now the wife of this rich Greek?
Farewell ! (*Starts away.*)

ZEN. (*Clinging to him.*)

Nay, Lysander, thou shalt not go! Hear me first,
Then, if thou wilt, condemn me!
By all the good within me do I swear
That, while my hand belongs to Draco,
My heart is truly thine!

· LYS.

But still thou art his wife!

ZEN.

'T is true, Lysander ; yet I do protest
'T was by no wish of mine.   My father,
For some purpose which I know not of,
Compelled my marriage with the Greek.
For months I struggled to escape,
And on my very knees implored release ;
The love I bore thee gave me strength,
But nothing could avail against his will.—

This mockery of marriage did prevail,
And Draco is, within the law, my lord;
But, while the fetters bind my hands,
They cannot bind my heart!

Lys.

Oh, that thy father were not thy father,
That I might reckon with him!

Zen,

Nay, my love, speak not against my sire.
He may have seen the future as we lovers see it
    not,
And in my marriage thus with Draco
Thought to keep me safe from harm.

Lys.

Then thou art content?

Zen.

Content, my love?
Content only as I lie within thine arms,
And feel thy kisses on my lips!
Content with Draco? A question thou doth ask
To which thy very self doth make reply!
Why art thou here to-night?—and why
Do I dishonor brave to meet thee?
Because I am content with Draco?
Ah, Lysander, how canst thou be so blind?

Lys.

No longer blind am I! Truth is in thine eyes,

And I know I am beloved!
———Now that I have found thee
I will not let thee go!

ZEN.

What wilt thou do?

LYS.

What wouldst thou have me do?

ZEN.

What thou wilt.

LYS.

Then, thou shalt depart with me!   In Phoenicia
Thou wilt forget thou ever had a father
Or an Athenian for thy husband.

ZEN.

Wherever thou goest, I will go with thee!

LYS.

Then come.

(*Lysander starts to exit centre, leading Zenobia by
the hand.   Diomed enters and confronts them.*)

DIO.

Stay!

ZEN.

My father!

Lys. (*Covering his face with his cloak.*)
Diomed !

Dio.

Who is this gay gallant who tempts thee
From thy duty as a wife—Marcius?
       (*Lysander uncovers his face.*)
Not Marcius?—who, then, is this?

Lys.

One who might teach thee duty to thy country
And justice to thy daughter!

Dio.

An insolent slave!

Lys.

Thou——— -

Zen.

Hush, Lysander—hush! Revile him not—
He is still my father.

Dio.

Ay, thy father—and thou the wife of Draco.
       (*Turning to Lysander.*)
So, thou art Lysander?

Lys.

Ashamed I never yet have been
To own my name. I am Lysander!

40

Zenobia : a Tragedy.

DIO. (*Starting toward exit, right.*)

A Phoenician!—an enemy to Attica!
A spy! What, ho! the watch!
(I'll have thee apprehended !)
What, ho! the watch!

(*Lysander draws his sword and bars the way.
Zenobia springs between them.*)

ZEN.

Lysander! father! Diomed!
Wilt thou make thy daughter's heart bleed more?
And thou, Lysander, wouldst thou kill my sire?

DIO.

What, ho!—the watch! Treachery!
What, ho! the watch!

(*Rushes toward opposite exit. Lysander follows,
brandishing his sword. Zenobia throws her
arms about Lysander's neck and restrains him.*)

ZEN.

Stay, Lysander, stay! Let not bloodshed
Mar the happiness of this night!
Get thou back to Marcius—quick—
Before my father can return,
And, if the gods so will, meet me here,
To-morrow night, at this same hour,
And by the stars above us do I swear
To follow thee where'er thou wilt!

Go, Lysander, and I will overtake my father,
Ere the guard is nigh, and give thee time
To get away from Athens.

LYS.

Then, to-morrow night, at this same time,
Come vict'ry or defeat, thou'lt find me here.
'Til then, farewell! (*Embraces her.*)

ZEN.

Farewell, Lysander!

LYS. (*As he exits centre.*)

Farewell!

ZEN.

Now must I find my father.
Father! Diomed! father! (*Runs off left.*)

———

SCENE 2–Before Draco's Tent, in the Grecian Camp, on the Hills
above the Plain of Marathon. Two Hours Later.

THEO. (*Entering with Philander, left.*)

This must, indeed, be Draco's camp,
And here, I take it, is his own marquee;
But, now I'm here, my courage fails,
And makes me fear my uncle.

PHIL.

Then take an humble slave's advice—
Bottle anger—throw jealousy to the winds—

Zenobia : a Tragedy.

Return to Athens, and—go to bed.

THEO.

Nay, nay, Philander, I'll never sleep again
Until the fickle heart of Marcius feels
The penalty of his treason.

PHIL.

Ah, well, a woman's way is not a man's way—
Nor a slave's way, either. My way lies yonder.
I'll leave thee to master Draco.

(*Starts to retire, right, and encounters Leonidas.*)

LEON.

Stay, slave! What brings thee hither?

PHIL.

That which hath taken many a wiser man
Hence and hither——a woman.

LEON. (*Looking at Theodosia, who hides her face.*)
A woman! Thou rogue—her name?

PHIL.

Now canst thou prove I am indeed a fool ;
I know her well, and yet her name I cannot say.
Ask her thyself, good soldier.

(*Leonidas advances to centre, thus barring the way
to the tent. Theodosia throws back her drapery.*)

LEON.

Theodosia! Sweet cousin, whither goest thou?

Zenobia : a Tragedy.

THEO.

To General Draco.

LEON.

To General Draco? 'T is a strange hour
To visit our uncle in camp.

THEO.

Still must I see him.

LEON.

I fear he'll not receive thee.

THEO.

He'll not refuse to see his niece.
Let me pass, Leonidas.

PHIL.

Ay, let us pass, Leonidas.

LEON. (*to Philander.*)

Slave! advance a step, and through thy body
Will I pass this good spear!

PHIL.

Then, indeed, will I be passed, and thereby
Saved the trouble of passing henceforward.

LEON.

Hold thy tongue, thou crack-brained babbler!

PHIL.

As thou wilt.   True philosophy teaches men—

44

And women, too, for that matter—
To bridle their tongues.

(*Puts dagger in his mouth.*)

Now, being bridled, wilt thou not say
I am a philosopher?

THEO.

Time flies!—precious minutes wasted!
Let us pass, Leonidas.

LEON.

Not 'til I know thy errand.

THEO.

Thou didst not treat me thus in Athens.

LEON.

I do but execute our uncle's orders.

THEO.

Once I thought thou didst care for me.

LEON.

Thou knowest I love thee.

THEO.

Then by that love I do implore thy help.
Take me to the General.   'T is
A matter which concerns him near.

LEON.

A matter that concerns our uncle?

Zenobia : a Tragedy.

THEO.

Also his wife—and—and Marcius.
Now wilt thou let me pass?

LEON.

Marcius and *Zenobia!*   This, then,
Concerns the *honor* of General Draco!
By Jupiter, thou *shalt* see our uncle!
But, stay a little.   I'll go within
And apprise him of thy coming.

(Leonidas enters tent.)

THEO.

   My courage rushes forth
Like water from a broken urn.
Would I could return to Athens,
And leave my tale untold.—
Have courage, wavering heart, and think
How nigh to thee is thy revenge!

(Re-enter Leonidas.)

LEON.

  Come, Theodosia.
Our uncle doth consent to see thee.

(Theodosia enters tent, and Leonidas exits right.)

PHIL.

Now, let designing lovers hide their faces,
For jealous Fury goes to shame the graces!

(Follows Leonidas off, right.)

Zenobia : a Tragedy.

DRA. (*as Theodosia enters.*)

Theodosia, my child, what brings thee here?

THEO.

Love—hate—both combined!   A devil's in me!
I come to have it exorcised!

DRA.

Thou must not speak in riddles.
I'll listen, but thou must be brief.

THEO.

I would speak of Marcius.

DRA.

Well, what of Marcius?
'T is sure no lover's quarrel brought thee here?

THEO.

You love Marcius?

DRA.

As my son.

THEO.

He is just—honest—true?

DRA.

I'll stake my life on it.
——But why this questioning?

THEO.

Marcius, the brave, the generous—

47

Zenobia : a Tragedy.

Marcius, the trusted friend of Draco,
Is a traitor!   Stay, do not speak :
I'll tell thee all—then mayest thou reply.
———A little while ago,
I saw them—Marcius———

DRA.

What's this to me?   Dost thou not know
I have no time to listen to such tales?
Tell me no more—I will not hear thee.

THEO.

Nay, but thou shalt—if thou dost regard
The honor of thy wife!

DRA.

Stop! I'll hear no more!

THEO.

And yet I will repeat the truth,
Tho' death repays my zeal.
Marcius loves thy wife, and she
Loves Marcius, and not thee!

DRA.

'Tis a lie!—I'll not believe it!
Go, child, go, lest I forget I am thy uncle!

THEO.

Not yet!   I'll tell thee all,
Then mayest thou exercise thy will—
Kill me, if thou must—I care not—

48

Zenobia : a Tragedy.

Life's not sweet.
       Not three hours since,
I saw them in thy garden. They met in the light,
Where both were plain in view,
Embraced each other, kissed, and parted,
But soon returned again, and for seeming hours,
Tho' the moments were but brief,
They talked of love and happy days
That might be theirs in other climes ;
And, as they talked, he kissed her—
Not alone upon her lips—
But on her eyes and cheeks and hair,
Whispering ever and anon
That all his soul belonged to her.

DRA.

No, no!—I'll not believe it!
'T was not Zenobia thou didst see ;
Thy woman's wit hath failed thee,
And thou wast deceived in the dark!
My wife untrue?　'T were infamy to believe it!

THEO.

They spoke of thee, and she, weeping,
Said that life was bitter, and that thou,
Her husband, had no place within her heart—
Her father forced the marriage—
And tho' her hand belonged to Draco,
Her heart belonged to him!

Zenobia : a Tragedy.

DRA.

Can this be true?   No, no!
And yet there stirs within me such a storm—
Such raging heat, such doubt, such damning pain,
Such jealous love, such haunting dread,
I dare not think, for fear that thought
May bring conviction!
      No, no, I'll not believe it!
I will not doubt the love of my Zenobia!
And Marcius false?—Marcius her lover?
Again I say I'll not believe it!

THEO.

Then thine eyes shall put my story to the proof!
'T is hardly midnight, and the morn
Will gleam above the eastern horizon
Ere Marcius takes his leave.
Come with me to Athens, and see
With thine own eyes the perfidy of Marcius and
     thy wife!

DRA.

No more can nature bear!   I would deny,
And yet my heart demands the proof !
Theodosia, I'll go with thee to Athens ;
If 't is true, I'll thank thee, tho'
It wrings my heart.   If false,
The gods protect thee!   If Zenobia is untrue,
And Marcius her lover, death will be bliss
Beside the torture I'll invent to wrack them!

Zenobia : a Tragedy.

But soft;
My head's on fire, and makes my heart unjust.
Zenobia is true—it must be so—and Marcius
Is my friend. And yet I'll go—
Not that I believe it—but so
I'll prove to thee thy story's false!
                Come, let us hence.

(*Starts toward entrance. Great commotion outside.
Leonidas rushes in.*)

LEON.

General, General, our outposts are attacked!

(*Exit Leonidas, running.*)

DRA. (*Donning helmet and girding on his sword.*)
The enemy here, and Marcius in Athens!
My heart's aflame with jealous love!
Zenobia false!—nestling in her lover's arms,
And I, her husband, called to battle,
With all this jealous doubt tugging at my heart!
I would return. My soul's in Athens,
Tho' my duty's here. I'll stay—the foe repulsed,
I'll go to find the traitor!

(*Rushes off. Clashing of swords outside, gradually
receding in the distance.*)

THEO.

What have I done? Oh, Marcius,
Thou art now undone, and I the jealous cause;
Thou didst scorn me, and I am revenged ;

51

Zenobia : a Tragedy.

And yet—strange is woman's inconsistency—
I never loved thee half so well as now.

(Falls upon couch, weeping.   Enter Marcius.)

MAR.

General! General!   *(Sees Theodosia.)*
What, Theodosia here?   Theodosia!
(She is silent.)   Theodosia!

THEO.

Yes, Marcius.

MAR.

What brings thee here to camp
At such a time of peril?

THEO.

Oh, ask me not—I would not have thee know.

MAR.

I thought I saw thee scarce three hours since
In Athens.   Thou didst make good haste.
'T is strange ; and yet I have no right to question
     thee.

(Enter Draco.)

DRA.

So, thou hast returned?
Why didst thou go to Athens to-night?

MAR.

To Athens?

Zenobia : a Tragedy.

DRA.

I would know what called thee there.

(*Marcius hesitates.*)

(*Aside.*) He is silent! He will not speak!
Then it is the truth!
(*Aloud.*) Marcius, look up—
It is thy more than father speaks—
Look up, and say thou art my friend—
That thou hast never been untrue—
That thou hast not been to-night in Athens—
That thou didst not meet my wife,
Nor speak to her as lovers speak,
Nor press her to thy heart, nor seek
To win her love from me—say it is a lie,
And tho' the proof be damning,
Yet will I believe thee!

MAR. (*Aside.*)

He thinks I am Zenobia's lover!

DRA.

On thy soul I bid thee speak!

MAR. (*Aside*)

What shall I say? For Zenobia's sake
I dare not tell the truth, and half the truth
Condemns me. If I answer him,
And tell of Zenobia's meeting with her brother,
I am forsworn, and she is lost ;
If I say I met her in the garden, and

Can give no reason, 't will but confirm
The jealous fears of Draco.

DRA. (*Impatiently.*)

Come, come—I wait for thee to speak!

MAR.

Alas! I cannot answer thee.

DRA.

Then thou art false!   Nay, more—
Thou art a traitor to thy country's cause!

MAR.

A traitor?

DRA.

Ay, traitor! There is a law in Attica which decrees
That he who leaves the camp upon the eve of
      battle
Shall pay forfeit with his life!
Thou art a traitor, and shalt die—
The law shall give me my revenge!

(*Rushes off.*)

MAR.

Is this a dream, and am I Marcius?
'T is indeed a nightmare, and when awake
I'll laugh to think of what I've seemed to suffer.
Alas, it is no dream—I am awake,
And what doth seem a dreadful vision
Is an all too true reality!

Zenobia : a Tragedy.

Guiltless tho' I am, for that dear lady's sake
I dare not speak.

       Ah, Zenobia, sad it were to think
That, while I may not speak, because
My promise binds, yet my silence cannot save
    thee ;
But thou wilt confess the truth, and thus
Thy honor and my fair reputation save ;
For tho' the law is stringent, and my act a crime,
Draco will shield me when he knows the truth.
——What spying eyes beheld me in the garden?
What sland'rous, lying tongue has brought
To Draco's ears the story of a false intrigue?
Oh, shame upon his venomed tongue!
May palsy seize upon his arm,
And Jupiter's thunderbolts blast his sight!
Had I the wretch before me now
The infernal powers of earth and air
Would not stay my hand!

        I'll go to Draco
And force from him the coward's name—
Once found, I'll kill him, tho' he be
My nearest kin!

       (*Starts toward entrance.*)

      THEO. (*Whispering.*)

Marcius——!

      MAR. (*Pausing.*)

Thou here yet?—I thought thou hadst gone

Zenobia : a Tragedy.

(*A sudden thought strikes him ; he gazes at Theodosia in horror, then shakes his head.*)

No, no, it cannot be!   And yet
Her coming here to-night, at such a time!—
It must be she!   Altho'
I'd rather death should strike me
Than to learn that Theodosia was so false!
——Theodosia, say it was not thou!

(*Theodosia springs from the couch, and falls on her
knees at his feet.*)

Speak, speak—I bid thee speak!

THEO.

Mercy—mercy--it was I!

MAR.

Thou, Theodosia?

THEO.

Yes ; I saw thee in the garden with Zenobia ;
I saw her kiss thee—saw her take thy hand—
And then, inspired by Diomed, came
And told the tale to Draco.

MAR.

And *thou* didst this—thou, Theodosia?
Oh, shame!   I'd rather see thee dead.

THEO.

Oh, Marcius, turn away thine eyes—
I cannot bear to feel them looking into mine.

Zenobia : a Tragedy.

I am too weak to face thee—on my soul
There rests the burden of my guilt!

MAR.

Ah, Theodosia!
Little dost thou know what thou hast done!
A soldier does not fear to die—
It is disgrace that wounds him most.

THEO.

Forgive me, Marcius ; I loved thee,
And my heart was filled with envy
When I saw thee with Zenobia.
My crime is black—but jealous love's the cause.
It is not modesty to speak, but speak I will—
I love thee, Marcius—I love but thee!

MAR.

Thou lovest me—*me*—Marcius?
Oh, say those words again—look up—
Give me thine eyes, and let me read within thy
        soul
That thou dost speak the truth!

THEO.

I love thee, Marcius ; it was my love
That brought me here.

MAR.

Thou lovest me?—thou, Theodosia—
The niece of Draco, and the sweetest maid

In all fair Athens? Ah, thou dost but jest with me.

THEO.

'T is true--I love thee—
Canst thou not see how much I love thee?

MAR.

The gods be praised!   A moment since
I could have slain thee ; now,
Altho' I know thy jealous heart
Has peril'd my life and stained a woman's honor,
Yet, is love so strange a thing,
I can forgive thee even this.   For, in truth,
I've always loved thee, tho' I did not dream
That thou couldst ever stoop to care for me.

THEO. (*Rising and throwing herself into his arms*)
Thou wilt forgive me?

MAR. (Kissing her.)

Already art thou forgiven.
I am condemned, and thou the cause,
But, tho' I die, my latest thought
Shall be for Theodosia!

(Enter Draco with guards.)

DRA.

There is the traitor—seize him!

(*Soldiers advance toward Marcius with extended
spears.   Theodosia bars the way.*)

Zenobia : a Tragedy.

Theo.

Stand back!   You shall not have him!
'T was I condemned him—let me die instead!

END OF SECOND ACT.

———

Zenobia : a Tragedy.

ACT III.

Scene 1—Before the Temple of Justice, Athens.   Soldiers Guarding Entrance. Mob Grouped About. Two Days Later.

First Soldier.

They say it fares ill with young Captain Marcius.

Second Soldier.

And ill be it, say I ;
A traitor's a traitor whoe'er he be.

Phil. (*Approaching from left.*)

'T is not every traitor receives his due ;
Thou art a traitor to thy captain, Marcius!

Second Soldier.

Rash slave, begone!   Jest not with free men.

Phil.

The wiser man am I.   I know I am a slave ;
Thou thinkest thou art a free man.

First Soldier.

Now, by m' life, he had thee there!

60

Zenobia : a Tragedy.

But 't is no time for jesting—
Here comes one from within.

(*Messenger approaches from temple.*)

What's new?

MESSENGER.

Question me not—I'm in much haste!

FIRST SOL.

What say the judges?

MES.

Well, have it then : they have agreed—
Marcius must die.   (*Exits right.*)

THE MOB.

The traitor dies!—death to all traitors!
Long live Athens and the Athenians!

FIRST SOL.

Disperse!—the judges come.

(*Soldiers force back the mob.   Judges come from
Temple of Justice, followed by Marcius, bound,
and surrounded by soldiers.   Draco comes last,
with his head bowed*)

MAR.

One moment, good friends —
Let me speak to Draco.

THE MOB.

Away with him!—away with the traitor!

Zenobia : a Tragedy.

DRA.

Nay, let him speak.—
What wouldst thou of me?

MAR.

Draco, thou hast done me wrong ;
I am no traitor, either to my country or to thee!
No terror has the thought of death,
And welcome would it be did I but know
Thy head and not thy heart condemned me.

DRA.

Thy silence hath condemned thee.

MAR.

Then farewell—thou hast murdered thy friend!

(*Soldiers resume march, and all exit right except
Draco and Philander.*)

DRA.

Now, to Zenobia's chamber,
To force confession from her guilty lips.

(*Exits left.*)

PHIL.

Now, let who will face Draco's rage—
The Tragic Muse still has the stage!

(*Follows Draco off, left.*

Zenobia : a Tragedy.

(*Zenobia, Lydia and other maids discovered. Lydia dressing Zenobia's hair. African slaves waving fans*)

ZEN. (*Reading letter, aside.*)

Sweet news! Lysander's safe!
And tho' another day must pass
Ere we may find a ship to take us hence,
The hours will glide away in happy expectation.

(*To Lydia.*)

Where is our good niece, Theodosia, to-day?

LYD.

A while since I saw her in the garden,
Looking sore distressed.

ZEN.

Poor niece—a sleepless night, perhaps—
Short dreams make heavy eyes.
So bright a morn as this
Should bring content to all the world.
Oh, content enough am I!

LYD.

And merry, too, my lady.

ZEN.

Ay, and merry! So merry,
I'd have thee sing some roundelay ;
But gay indeed must it be

63

Else will it not keep pace with my merry mood.

LYD.

A song of love?

ZEN.

Of love?—why not?
As there's no sorrow apart from love,
So there's no happiness without it.

LYD. (*Singing.*)

A butterfly said to her fluttering mate,
   "Oh, what is the secret of love?"
Her pretty spouse answered, "I really don't know;
   Go ask of our neighbor, the dove."
So the butterfly hurried away to the bird,
   And repeated her question there:
The dove made reply, with a tremulous sigh,
   "Go ask of the maiden fair--
      Go ask of the maiden fair."

The butterfly sought for the maiden so fair,
   And perched on her dainty white glove,
She murmured in accents as light as the air,
   "Won't you tell me the secret of love?
On the cheeks of the maid came a delicate flush,
   As pink as the breast of the dove--
"When your lips feel the bliss of a true lover's kiss,
   You will know the secret of love--
      You will know the secret of love!"

(*Enter Draco, centre.*)

DRA.

Begone—all of you begone! all save thy mistress;
I'd speak with her alone!

(*All exit centre except Draco and Zenobia.*)

So, thou guilty woman,

Zenobia : a Tragedy.

All the love thou promised me was false!

Zen.

(*Aside.*)   Marcius has betrayed me!
(*Aloud.*)   Thou art cruel and unjust--
I will not stay to hear thee.

(*She attempts to leave the room, but Draco bars
the way.*)

Dra.

Thou shalt not only stay, but thou
Shalt also listen to the outraged words
Of a most wronged husband!
          ——Woman, I know thy lover!

Zen.

'T is false!   I have no lover—
None save thee—my husband.

Dra..

Forswear thyself no more :
A fool was I, and blind as well ;
But eyes, once opened, will not sleep again!

Zen. (*Attempting to caress him*)

Indeed, my lord, thou art misinformed.
What wicked tongue has come
Between me and my love—my husband?

Dra.

I will not listen!—-thou art false!

(*Aside.*)   And yet, suppose it was a lie?
What if my wife is true,
And loves me as I thought of old?
(*Aloud.*)   Zenobia, tell me truly,
Have I done thee wrong,
And dost thou love thy husband?

ZEN. (*Embracing him.*)
Should not a woman love her lord?
(*Shouts of mob outside.*)
What's that?
DRA. (*Musingly.*)
They take him away to die.

ZEN.
Who, my lord?
DRA.
The man they call thy lover.

ZEN. (*Aside.*)
Lysander! Oh, pitiful gods,
Look down in mercy!
(*Aloud.*)   My lord, my lord, I would go hence!

DRA.
Wherefore? Here is thy husband—
Is not thy place with him?

(*Commotion continues.*)

ZEN.
My lord, my lord, I pray thee let me go.

Zenobia : a Tragedy.

(*Aside.*) Lysander, my love, my love!
(*Aloud*) Oh, I would be gone!

(*Rushes toward centre door. Draco seizes her by the wrists.*)

DRA.

And I would have thee stay!
What's to thee the death of one
That rumor *falsely* calls thy lover?

(*Tumult increases, and Zenobia struggles frantically to release herself.*)

ZEN.

Let me go! My lord, let me go!—
'T is torture here!

DRA.

Then—then he is thy lover?
Speak, woman, speak—he is thy lover?

ZEN. (*Still struggling to escape.*)

No——yes—— no, no, no!
Yes——yes——my lord!

(*Falls on her knees.*)

I confess the truth—but spare his life!
—If thou didst ever pity feel, I pray thee
Feel it now, and save my love!

DRA.

Spare thy lover, guilty woman?—no!

A thousand deaths like his would not atone
For all the wrong that he and thou have done me!
Death for thy lover!—worse for thee!

(*Pushes her away, and turns to leave room. She
clasps him about body and drags after him.*)

ZEN.

Spare me not, my lord—but spare my love!
My guilty life is thine to take—
Slay *me*, and let my death suffice for both!

(*Draco draws dagger, catches her by the arm ; then
roughly throws her aside. She falls to the floor,
insensible.*)

DRA.

No, no, not yet—she is my wife—
I loved her once—I love her even now!

(*Rushes off centre*)

———

SCENE 3--Corridor in Draco's Palace.

PHIL. (*Entering with Lydia, right.*)

Hi! ho! Things have reached a pretty pass—
There's fiercer war within fair Athens
Than was ever known without.

LYD.

Woe the day! Poor my lady!
What evil tongue hath brought about
So dread a time?

Zenobia : a Tragedy.

PHIL.

I know not—so I forbear to speak.
Gossips tell all they know—therefore,
Did I know, I'd tell thee.

LYD.

Here comes Draco, and with him
Diomed, the merchant.   Let's go.

PHIL.

With all my heart—seeing
Thou hast my heart, and thou art going.

(*Both exit left, as Draco and Diomed enter right.*)

DRA.

Out on thee, thou trading hypocrite—
Out on thee, and all thy brood!
Thy daughter's false, and so art thou!
Get thee gone, lest I do thee some injury!

DIO. (*Sneering.*)

Has my lord taken leave of his wits
That he should thus turn upon his friends?

DRA.

Friends?—I have no friends!
My wife's untrue--Marcius is false—
What other friends have I?

DIO.

Thou dost forget me.

Zenobia : a Tragedy.

DRA.

Falser art thou than all the rest :
Get thee gone, I say—get thee gone!

DIO.

I'll not be gone!   If so
Thou do thy worst, thou canst but kill—
My sweet revenge remains to torture thee ;
For, let me tell thee, Draco,
Long ago I plotted for this hour.
Know me now—not as Diomed, the Phoenician,
But as Thisbian, who, when thou and I were
      young,
Loved the maid that thou by trickery won!
I swore that day to pay thee dear ; and so I have ;
For she thou callest now thy wife,
Altho' my daughter, is a Syrian slave—
I bought her mother in the market place at Sidon!
—I waited 'til thy wife had died, and then
I had thee give thy name to this young slave.
I knew she loved another, and would bring
Dishonor on thy house.   Thou canst not say
I have not plotted well!

   DRA. (*Drawing dagger and stabbing Diomed.*)
Die—die—thou plotting hypocrite!

(*Diomed staggers, then grapples with Draco, and
      both struggle off left.*)

Zenobia : a Tragedy.

(*Zenobia still lying on the floor. Marcius rushes in, bareheaded, with his tunic torn and bloodstained, and grasping sword.*)

MAR.

The vampires! For a brief space
I.have escaped them! 'If I can but find Zenobia,
All may yet be well!

(*Sees Zenobia.*)

Zenobia! Zenobia!

(*Raises her, and her head falls back.*)

Ah! gods! she is dead!—I am lost!——

(*Zenobia revives.*)

No--she lives! she lives!--I may yet be saved!

ZEN. (*Whispering..*)

Lysander—Lysander!

MAR.

She speaks of her brother.—
'T is not Lysander, but I—Marcius.

ZEN. (*Slowly rising.*)

'T is thou? Oh, Marcius,
How couldst thou be so false to me?

MAR.

False, Zenobia?

71

Zenobia : a Tragedy.

ZEN.

My husband's learned the truth,
And none but thou didst know it.
—Marcius, my lover is condemned to die!

MAR.

Thy *lover?*

ZEN.

Yes, Marcius.   Forgive me—
Lysander is no brother, but my love ;
And now, too late, I see the peril
That my folly brought him to.
Marcius, good Marcius, wilt thou not save him?

MAR.

Thy lover, Zenobia, is safe
And many leagues from Athens.   'T is I
Who am condemned, and only now
Escaped the soldiers and the mob.
They say—oh, pardon me, my lady—
They say I am thy lover, and because
I left the camp upon the eve of battle
The law's invoked to give to me a traitor's death!

ZEN. (*Aside.*)

Lysander's safe!   My love is safe!
(*To Marcius.*)   But thou, my Marcius, what
A wretched plight has all my scheming
Brought thee to!   Thou art condemned to die?

Zenobia : a Tragedy.

MAR.

Yes ; naught but my heels
And this good blade have saved me.
(*Shouts of mob outside.*)
Hark! the rabble and the soldiers come—
Thirsting like vampires for my blood!

ZEN.

No, my Marcius, it must not be—
I will confess, and thus shall save thee.

(*Great commotion and roar of voices.*)

MAR.

They are at the gate!

ZEN.

Fly, Marcius, fly, ere it be too late!

MAR.

I cannot leave thee to the fury of the mob!

ZEN.

I do not fear—they would not dare
To harm the wife of General Draco.

MAR.

I am a soldier, though condemned to die,
And soldiers fight when cowards run away!

ZEN.

Thou art no coward ; still
Must thou be gone.   Think of Theodosia—

Think of those thou lovest.   Quick—be gone!
And if the Fates be kind enough to spare us all,
At even post thyself within the shadow of the
    wall,
Where thou Lysander brought to me;
There will I send to thee thy love—
There will Theodosia surely find thee!

MAR.

My heart is filled with anguish—wavering
'Twixt my honor and my love for Theodosia!
But—away with love when honor is at stake;
I'll tarry with thee tho' it cost my life!

THE MOB. (*Outside.*)

Marcius!   Where is the traitor, Marcius?

(*Enter Theodosia, left.*)

THEO.

Marcius! Marcius! I thank the gods I find thee
    safe!
(*They embrace.*)   What's that noisy tumult?

ZEN.

The mob—they seek my life!

(*Roar of voices gradually grows louder, until mob
    and soldiers burst into the room, and rush
    toward Marcius.   Theodosia springs between
    him and the rabble.*)

THEO.

Stand back!   What want you here?

THE MOB.

The traitor, Marcius!

THEO.

He is no traitor!
'T was I whose words condemned him!
In jealous rage I told the tale
That did excite my uncle's wrath.
He is my lover, and a truer soldier
Never fought for Athens.

THE MOB.

He's a traitor!   Death to the traitor!

MAR.

Then come and fight—for fight you must—
Alive you shall not take me!

THEO.

No, no, dear Marcius—fly!
Think how little thy single arm can do
          Against so many!

          (*Mob presses forward.*)

ZEN. (*Advancing.*)

Stand back!   'T is I, Zenobia,
The wife of General Draco, speaks!
Stand back! or on your heads shall fall

Zenobia : a Tragedy.

The severest penalty of the law!

THE MOB.

We want Marcius—give us Marcius!

ZEN.

If ye be men, begone!
Before the sun above us do I swear
That he you seek is innocent!

THE MOB.

Kill him—kill the traitor!

(Enter Draco, left, flourishing sword.)

DRA. (*To mob*)

Hold! I, Draco, command it!
'T is I who shall be judge and executioner!

(Turning to Marcius.)

So, thou traitor, thou hast escaped, and with
Thine oath of innocence still upon thy lips,
Thou hast returned to see my wife again!
Ingrate that thou art, defend thyself!

*(Rushes at Marcius and attempts to run him through
with his sword. Marcius acts on the defensive.)*

MAR.

Draco, hear me ere thou dost strike!

DRA.

I'll hear thee--yes! but not until thy dead lips

76

Zenobia : a Tragedy.

Speak the expiation thy crime deserves!

(*Draco continues his attack, and Marcius, acting
upon the offensive, disarms him. He is about
to kill Draco, but suddenly draws back, and
throws away his sword.*)

MAR.

Take thy life—I cannot slay thee!

(*Draco picks up sword, and runs at Marcius again.*)

Here is my breast!   Do with me as thou wilt!

DRA.

Then——die! as thou dost deserve!

(*Thrusts at Marcius, but Zenobia springs forward
and seizes his arm.*)

ZEN.

Spare him, Draco—spare him!
I love another—'t is not Marcius!

DRA.

Another lie! guilty woman, be not more forsworn!

THEO.

She speaks the truth—I was misled—
Marcius is innocent!

DRA.

Mystery upon mystery!   What means it all?
Have I then wronged thee, Marcius?

—·But thou, false woman, what other love hast
    thou?

ZEN.

Oh, let me not speak more! Let it suffice
I give my live to save the one
My scheming cost so dear!

DRA.

Tell me thy lover's name!

ZEN.

I will not—nor hast thou power to make me!

DRA.

Then, before these men of Athens
Will I force from thee thy secret!

ZEN.

Do thy worst—I'll still defy thee!

DRA. (*Rushing at Marcius again.*)

Then it *is* Marcius ; thy silence convicts him!

ZEN.

Stay, Draco, stay—I'll tell thee all!
Know, if thou must, I never loved thee—
All my life I've loved another—
A gallant soldier, tho' he fights for Persia!
'T was he I met within the garden—
He who held me in his arms, and swore
He'd take me far away from Athens!

Zenobia : a Tragedy.

For my father's sake I wed thee, Draco ;
I scorned thee then—I loathe thee now ;
And tho' my love's decreed my shame,
That shame is sweet—I glory in it!

DRA.

Thou art no wife of mine!   Thou art a slave!
I bought thee from that trading hypocrite
Who called himself thy father!

ZEN.

My father! where is my father?

DRA.

Where thou wilt find him when thy soul goes
        hence!

ZEN.

My father dead? Monster, thou hast killed him!
        Come! complete thy work!

DRA.

Not yet ; 't will be a sweeter sight
To see thee suffer! Before these citizens of Athens
Will I brand thee as a slave!

(*Seizes red-hot iron from a brazier, and catches
    Zenobia by the arm.   She shrieks and struggles
    to escape.   One of the mob throws back his
    hood and cloak, revealing the garb of a Persian
    soldier, who springs to Zenobia's side, pushes
    Draco back, and folds her in his arms.*)

Zenobia : a Tragedy.

ZEN.

Lysander! Why hast thou come here, Lysander?

LYS.

To save thee, or to perish with thee!

DRA.

So, this is thy lover—a Persian spy!
Seize him! seize him!

(*Lysander springs forward, sword in hand, and
faces the mob and soldiers. They beat him
down and trample him to death, and then sur-
round Zenobia.*)

DRA.

Hold! Death's too sweet a boon
For such as she! Slave that she is,
Her fate shall be the block!
To the mart with her—to the slave mart!
He who has the gold shall have her!

ZEN. (*Drawing dagger.*)

Back! stand back—all of you!
This dagger in my thrice-nerved hand
Is poisoned with the deadly venom of the asp :
'T is death to he who touches me!

(*All fall back, and Zenobia throws herself upon her
knees beside Lysander.*)

ZEN.

Lysander, dear, I thought to find

Zenobia : a Tragedy.

A happier recompense than this;
But 't is sweeter than another parting!
    Look thou here, good Marcius—
Here's my love! Is he not fair?
Were not these bleeding hands a hero's?
Did not these matted curls o'ertop the brow
Of one who, had he not been mortal,
Would have been a god? Could I
Have known this man and not have loved him?

Mar.

Poor lady—poor lady!

Zen.

Wilt thou not forgive me, Marcius—
And thou, Theodosia?

Mar.

I forgive thee, as I hope for pardon
From thy much-wronged husband.

Theo.

This sad ending does, like a mantle,
Cover the errors of thy heart.

Dra.

Again, I say, to the mart with her—
To the slave mart!

Zen. (*Rising and standing erect.*)

I am no slave—nor will I be!

Zenobia : a Tragedy.

I hurl defiance at thee, Draco,
And go to join Lysander!

(*Stabs herself, and falls dead across Lysander's body.
Lydia comes running on from left, followed by
Philander.*)

LYD.

Oh, my poor, dear mistress!

PHIL.

Here's the penalty of love's designing—
The lovers dead, and all the rest repining.

END OF PLAY.

———

A Confederate Episode.

A DETAIL FROM THE BATTLE OF FRANKLIN, TENN.,
Nov. 3o, 1864.

There was joy in the heart of farmer Brent,
Tho' his eyes were dim and his figure bent,
For Hood was marching, day and night,
To put the troops of the North to flight—
Up from the banks of the Tennessee,
With horse, and foot, and artillery.
      But it wasn't of Hood alone he thought—
Of Hood and the battles yet unfought—
But the boys he had sent away to the war,
Who were coming back with brigade and corps,
To fight for the South, and for Hood and Lee,
In their native valleys of Tennessee.
The mother had died while the boys were young,
When the hearts of the people were yet unwrung,
By the news of battle—the bitter strife
Of a struggle that threatened the nation's life ;
But the farmer was father and mother in one,
And he loved them each as an only son ;

A Confederate Episode.

And, strange to say, as the years rolled by,
And the whitening hair and vacant eye
Told that the days were nearly spent
In the quiet life of farmer Brent,
The love he had given his boys of old
Came back with interest a hundredfold,
And it never occurred to Joe and Ned
To grieve the heart or bow the head
Of the patient father, whose gentle ways
Had smoothed the troubles of childhood days.
 When the war broke out, and the message came
That North and South were all aflame,
And the guns that told of Sumter's fall
Made the Southern cause the cause of all,
The youth and brawn of Tennessee,
The merchants' sons and the yeomanry,
Went off to the front, with courage high,
To strive for glory—perhaps to die;
And, whenever a company marched away,
With waving colors and trumpet bray,
The Brent boys looked with sinking heart—
They wanted to go, but they couldn't depart,
And leave for their father's aged hands
The care of stock and harvest lands.
    And so they stayed, but the news that came
Back from the front, where the "rebel" name
Was filling the North with fear and dread,
And vict'ry perched where Southron led,
Touched their pride, and a blush of shame

A Confederate Episode.

More than once on their faces came
When the old folks looked their way, and said,
With quavering voice and nodding head,
That "feeding cattle and raising corn
Was women's work, when the land was torn
By the storm of battle, and, day by day,
The ranks were thinning, and thousands lay
Dead in the trenches, and General Lee
Was calling the youth and the chivalry
Of all fair Dixie, near and far,
To hurry on to the seat of war!"

But, while they suffered and said no word,
The soul of the father was being stirred
By the news of battle, and his brave old heart
Was sorely troubled, for he couldn't take part;
And then he looked at Ned and Joe,
And cried : "I'll do it—I'll let them go,
For they are young, and their limbs are free,
And they'll fight for the South as well as me!"

So the Brent boys gallantly marched away,
With waving colors and trumpet bray,
And the old man thought, "If either one
Should fall in battle, God's will be done."
But every letter that found its way
To farmer Brent was sure to say
That both the boys were sound and well,
With never a scratch from shot or shell;
And the tales they told of bravery done

A Confederate Episode.

By Franklin boys, in battles won,
Was a source of pride, for well he knew
Where others went his boys went too.
And yet, in spite of his heart and will,
'T was wearisome waiting at home until
The noise of battle, the leaden rain,
Should cease, and his boys come back again.

But now he went about the place
With peace in his heart and hope in his face;
And, whenever he passed the time of day
With friend or neighbor, he'd stop and say,
"What's the news of the boys in gray,
And what's the chance of 'em coming this way?"
And when they replied, as he knew they would,
"They were coming that way, 't was understood,"
He'd rub his hands, and say with a smile,
" Then I'll see my boys in a little while!"

Away to the South, where the boys in gray
Pressed eagerly forward, night and day,
Burning to match their might and skill
With the Federal troops at fair Nashville,
There was many a soldier lad who'd boast
To his bold companions up from the coast,
" This is my state, boys—keep your eyes on me,
And see how we fight in old Tennessee!"
But there wasn't a soldier in all the crowd
Who looked so brave, or who felt so proud,

A Confederate Episode.

As the Brent boys did on that fatal day
When the news came back that the Federals lay,
Entrenched in force, on hill and down,
To bar the way to Franklin town.

    In the early morn, when the boys awoke,
They could see the spires and curling smoke
Of the pretty town, and nearer still could plainly
    trace
The gabled roof of their native place :
And the sight of the homestead nestling there,
With the hills about it, green and fair,
Touched their hearts with a sudden thrill,
Like the echo of music when the night is still—
A feeling of pleasure, and yet of dread,
For the dear old place and its honored head.

    But scant was the time for hope or fear,
With the sun awake and the "yankees" near ;
And loud and shrill came the trumpet call—
"Forward, forward, one and all!"
Like a roar from the depths of a muffled mine,
A shout went up from the "rebel" line,
And like a torrent, wild and free,
The troops swept on toward the enemy.

    In the Federal ranks, beyond the trees,
Where the stars and stripes waved in the breeze,
The soldiers stood, with bated breath,
In silence, and as grim as death ;

A Confederate Episode.

While ever onward came the swell,
And higher rose the "rebel" yell!

But see! a sudden tremor seems to thrill
The Federal ranks along the hill—
A single shot—a ringing shout—
And then the fires of hell break out!
Under the storm of leaden rain
The Southrons pause, then charge again,
Until, within the jaws of death,
They feel the cannons' heated breath,
And then, and not 'til then, give way,
And Federal bullets win the day.

And now, where but an hour ago,
The waving grass was wont to grow,
The field has turned from green to red,
Where lie the dying and the dead ;
While, far away, the victor's shout
Proclaims defeat and Southron rout.

In the angle of an orchard wall,
Among the first that day to fall,
Torn and mangled in the fray,
Side by side the Brent boys lay.
With clasping hands, in sight of home,
They waited for the end to come ;
And then a wish, a burning thought,
Within their hearts expression sought—

A Confederate Episode.

If, in that hour of awful pain,
They could but see the place again—
Could see their father, waiting nigh,
And say a loving last good-bye!

———

Out from the bloody angle red
They pick their way among the dead,
Step by step, with reeling brain,
Fainting now, then up again,
'Til, stumbling on, they reach the bridge
And mount the old, familiar ridge.
With gaping wounds and gasping breath,
And eyes that have the hue of death,
They stagger up, and looking 'round
Survey the well-remembered ground—
The apple grove, the pebbled stream,
The scene of many a boyhood dream ;
The ivied-mill, where many an hour
They watched the slowly-grinding flour ;
The "quarters," where in lazy ease
The negroes sang their melodies ;
But where's the homestead, quaint and still?
And where's the barn beneath the hill?
Unroofed, with battered walls, and torn,
The dear old house where they were born,
And where the cattle once were fed
Is naught but wreck and embers red ;
While e'en the fence, where years ago
The old red gate swung to and fro,

A Confederate Episode.

Splintered by shell, and rent by ball,
Totters in ruins, ripe to fall.
     One look at the place so desolate,
A sob for the loving father's fate,
And then, "Farewell, old home!" they cried,
And, falling prostrate, gasped and died.

At even, as the sun went down
Behind the spires of Franklin town,
An aged farmer made his way
Among the dead who fell that day—
Bowed with grief, and dreading lest
He'd find his boys among the rest—
And climbing up the orchard hill
He found them lying, cold and still,
With rigid limbs, but wistful face,
Turned toward their native place.

Wayside Flowers.

IN BOHEMIA.

"I'd rather live in Bohemia than any other land."
JOHN BOYLE O'REILLY.

I'd rather live in Bohemia
   Than in any other land,
Where every man is a brother,
   With his heart in his open hand;
And whether a man be rich or poor,
   So long as his heart is right,
He's just as good in Bohemia-land
   As a king in his royal might.

Afar in a distant country
   A dreamer wandered alone;
His heart was heavy with yearning
   For the sound of a friendly tone;
He longed for the voice fraternal—
   For the touch of a kindly hand—
And, lo! he awoke one morning,
   And there was Bohemia-land.

In the beautiful valley beneath him,
　As the vapors rolled away,
He saw the City of Friendship—
　His vision of yesterday ;
And the heart of the weary dreamer
　Was filled with a joy divine :
" The world may do as it wills," he said,
　"Since love and content are mine."

So here's to the voice of friendship,
　And here's to the helping hand,
And here's to the sun of Bohemia
　That kisses the dreamer's land!

———

CISSY CLARE.

"If ever I marry a horrid man
　I hope to die as soon as I can !"
　　Thus said Cissy Clare.
And the sun came down with brightest ray
And kissed her cheeks that summer day,
　　And golden made her hair.

Over the hills came Billee Gray,
From a country village far away,
　　To woo sweet Cissy Clare.
He looked upon her roguish face,
And fell a prey to her airy grace,
　　And loved he Cissy Clare.

Wayside Flowers.

He fetched her posies every day—
He drove her other beaux away—
    But to speak he didn't dare;
But eyes said things that lips could not,
And go away he fain would not—
    Away from Cissy Clare.

At last, when flowers bloomed again
Beneath the Queen of Summer's reign,
    And the days were sweet and fair,
He took her hand with a soft caress,
And said in tones of tenderness,
    "I love thee, Cissy Clare!"

"Wilt go with me, my bonnie maid,
And see the parson now," he said—
    "'T is not so far away."
Then paled her face like highland snow,
And spake she bitterly and low,
    "I *cannot* marry, Billee Gray."

"I've made a dreadful vow," said she,
"And nevermore shall I be free,"
    Said pretty Cissy Clare.
"'If ever I marry a man,' said I,
'As soon as I can I hope I may die!'"
    And weep did Cissy Clare.

"You need not marry me," said he,
"But I, forsooth, will marry thee,
    My charming Cissy Clare."

Then smiling grew her face, and bright,
And, somehow, in the summer light
   His arm went 'round the golden hair.

———

MIDNIGHT.

Midnight! the bell tolls out the solemn hour ;
   Across the moorland and the vale,
   Across the mountain and the dale,
It rings with sweet, majestic power.

One! two! with intonation loud and deep
   Its chiming music seems to say,
"Sleep safely on until the day,
For I will o'er thee vigil keep!"

Three! four! upon the startled silence ring :
   A weary soul takes eagle flight
   To soar above in realms of light,
And heavenly voices sing.

Five! Six! oh, what a thrill
   It seems to waft far o'er the deep,
   As tho' 't would waken from their sleep
The silent forms so cold and still.

Seven! eight! a robber shudders at his toil ;
   For to his startled soul the bell
   Is ringing out his own death knell,
His wicked deeds to foil.

Nine! ten! upon the air the echoes swell,
    Then, rich with music, die away ;
    The watchman's weary footsteps stay,
And loud he thunders, "All is well!"

Eleven! twelve! at last 't is o'er ;
    The night wind rushes by and sighs,
    The fleeting echo swells and dies—
Then all is silent as before.

———

THE EDITOR.

With shuffling feet on the creaking floor,
    And a thoughtful look in his cold, gray eyes,
To the dingy realm of the compositor
    The stooping form of the editor hies.

A suggestion here, a misprint there,
    Or a dash that is out of place—
A letter or line that looks can spare,
    And a "cap" with a battered face.

Perhaps a line from a tardy friend
    Must be squeezed in the form some way ;
Or the "leader" the editor would extend
    With thoughts that have come to-day.

Oh, mystic realm of type and pen ;
    Oh, home of the thoughts that stay ;
Oh, potent molder of plastic men ;
    Oh, king of the modern day—

Wayside Flowers.

Thy mission lies in the path of fate ;
    Thy calling is one from God—
And the press shall praise with its endless life
    The editor under the sod.

THE "COMP." MAN AND THE POET.

Frank Stanton sez to me, sez he,
"'Pears like I never *did* git t' see
    Th' las' show was here, 'cause he,
    (Th' comp. man,) wa' no ways free
Wi' tickets, like show folks ustah be."

Sez I, "I reckon I kin fix it so
Yo'-all kin git t' see th' show—
    With a' extry seat on the lowes' row,
    Ez clos' t' th' rings ez yo'r 'lowed t' go,
'Les' yo'r travelin' wi' th' show."

An' Frank, he sez, with a smile, sez he,
"I reckon that 'u'd jest suit me,
    For there's nothin' in Georgy I'd ruther see
    Than a circus show—when seats ur free :
When yo' all reckon th' show 'll be?

---

www.ingramcontent.com/pod-product-compliance
Lightning Source LLC
Chambersburg PA
CBHW020029030726
47499CB00007B/2338